The Halloween Performance

Felicia Bond

SCHOLASTIC INC.

New York   Toronto   London   Auckland   Sydney

ISBN 0-590-43688-0

Copyright © 1983 by Felicia Bond.
All rights reserved. Published by Scholastic Inc., 730 Broadway, New York, NY 10003, by arrangement with Harper & Row, Publishers Inc.

12 11 10 9 8 7 6 5 4 3 2 1   0 1 2 3 4 5/9

Printed in the U.S.A.   23

First Scholastic printing, September 1990

TO MARILYN KRINEY

It was three days before Halloween,

and Roger's class was

giving a play in honor of the event.

Every day the class practiced,

over and over,

to get everything just right.

Invitations were made in school,

and families from all over town were invited.

The night of the performance,

the auditorium was packed.

Roger stood backstage.

He had a small but important role.

When the curtain opened,

sixteen mice danced onto the stage.

In the light of the moon,

they leaped and twirled

and sang.

There was plenty of talent.

The play was very funny,

and the audience laughed

when they were supposed to.

Roger listened closely
from behind the curtain.

His part was coming up.

Three more lines,

then two,

then one,

and Roger was on.

The audience applauded wildly

as the mice danced around

their Halloween pumpkin.

Everyone took a modest bow,

and the curtain closed.

Before he went to bed that night,

Roger's father took a picture of him.

But Roger

didn't need a picture

to remember.